the
LITTLE SOUL
and the EARTH
I'm Somebody!

A Children's Parable
Adapted from *Conversations with God*

NEALE DONALD WALSCH
Illustrated by Frank Riccio

HAMPTON ROADS
PUBLISHING COMPANY, INC.

for the evolving human spirit

Cover design by Frame25 Productions

Hampton Roads Publishing Company, Inc.
1125 Stoney Ridge Road
Charlottesville, VA 22902

434-296-2772
fax: 434-296-5096
e-mail: hrpc@hrpub.com
www.hrpub.com

If you are unable to order this book from your local
bookseller, you may order directly from the publisher.
Call 1-800-766-8009, toll-free.

Library of Congress Cataloging-in-Publication Data

Walsch, Neale Donald.
  The little soul and the earth : a children's parable from
Conversations with God / Neale Donald Walsch ; with illustrations by Frank Riccio.
     p. cm.
  Sequel to: Little soul and the sun.
  Summary: Little Soul is sent by God to embark on a series of
adventures on earth, the first of which is to be born.
  ISBN 1-57174-451-7 (alk. paper)
 [1. Spiritual life--Fiction. 2. God--Fiction. 3. Guardian
angels--Fiction.
4. Parables.] I. Riccio, Frank, ill. II. Walsch, Neale Donald.
Conversations with God. III. Title.
  PZ7+
  [E]--dc22
                              2005005342

ISBN 13: 978-1-57174-451-7

10 9 8 7 6 5 4 3 2

Printed on acid-free paper in China

To all the Little Souls everywhere,
which means, to every one of us.
For we, each of us, are Little Souls,
embraced by the Big Soul that we call God.
May we feel that embrace every day,
and may the stories of the Little Soul
open our hearts to sharing that embrace
with others.

—NDW

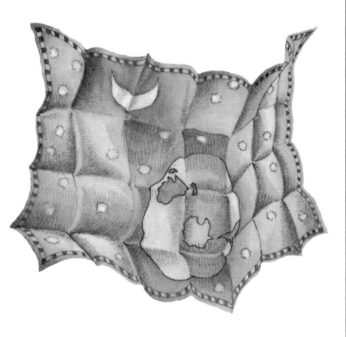

To the little ones.
You are our inspiration,
our treasure.

—FR

Dear Parents,
 and All Lovers of Children:

The parable of *The Little Soul and the Sun* has touched thousands of people around the world, treasured by parents and children alike. The response to that wonderful story has been so extraordinary that we began receiving requests for more of the same. "Why do the adventures of the Little Soul have to end here?" people asked.

Well, of course, they don't, and so those adventures now continue. The story in this book gives children a new way of looking at God, at life on Earth and its purpose, at how we create things in our lives, and at the wonderful experience called love. The tale here also shows that we are not our bodies; a body is something we have, not something we are.

If you believe these are important things for children to understand, and that there is no easier way to lead them to understanding than through a sweet story, you will be as happy that you found this book as we are that we produced it. You will also be happy to know that more of this same kind of energy may be found on the special Children's Page at www.nealedonaldwalsch.com.

There are few enough resources for parents these days as we seek to bring our children new and expanded ideas about God and about each other. So we decided to create this new series of illustrated storybooks for children as a partial remedy for that, and we are excited to be doing so.

Thank you for loving your children enough to bring them the story on these pages.

Neale Donald Walsch
Ashland, Oregon
April 2005

1

ONCE UPON NO TIME there was a Little Soul who said to God, "I don't want to leave you."

"Good!" God said with a big smile, "because you don't ever have to."

But the Little Soul did not understand, because this was the very day on which the Little Soul was going to be born, and the Little Soul thought that when you are born, you leave Heaven. In fact, the Little Soul was already standing in line, only a few steps away from the Doorway to Earth.

"Should I be afraid?" the Little Soul asked.

"No, no, no," God said, smiling again. "In fact, this is a day to be happy! This is your birthday!"

"I know," the Little Soul cried, "but it's also the day that I'll be leaving you, and saying goodbye to Heaven, and that makes me sad."

God gave the Little Soul a big hug. "I'll be with you always. It's impossible to leave me because I'm with you wherever you go."

"You are?" asked the Little Soul, eyes wide with hope.

And God answered immediately, "Yes, I am! All you have to do if you want me is call out to me, and you'll see that I'll always be there."

"Uh, what if things don't go right?" the Little Soul asked, starting to tremble. "I mean, 'Always' is a long time. What if I mess up? Will you still be there, or will you be mad and stay away?"

"Of course not," God answered, smiling. "I will never be mad at you. Why would I be mad just because you made a mistake? Everybody makes mistakes."

"Even you?" the Little Soul wanted to know.

"Well," God laughed, "there is asparagus . . ."

The Little Soul was feeling better already. "Okaay! So you'll be around all the time. That's good to know. That's almost like being in Heaven."

God smiled. "It IS being in heaven! You can't LEAVE Heaven because Heaven is the only thing I ever created! Heaven is everywhere you go."

"Even on Earth? Can I be in Heaven on Earth?"

Now there was a twinkle in God's eye. "Especially on Earth. Earth is one of the most wonderful places IN Heaven!"

"Then," said the Little Soul, "I'm ready to go. This is going to be fun!"

"Yes, it is," God agreed. "More fun than you know. And don't worry about a thing. Even if you forget what I told you, even if you forget about me, you'll have a very special friend to help you."

The Little Soul was shocked. "Forget about YOU? How could anybody forget about God?"

"Oh," God smiled, "you'd be surprised. Some people forget about me over and over, and almost everybody forgets about me once or twice."

"Well, I won't!" declared the Little Soul solemnly. "I'll NEVER forget about you."

God said, "That's very nice, but don't worry if you do. You'll always have Melvin."

"Melvin? Who's Melvin?" the Little Soul asked.

"Your very special friend! Melvin is an angel who has agreed to be with you all of your life, so that no matter what happens, you'll have someone to help you."

"Wow," said the Little Soul, "an angel who guards you."

"That's right!" God said. "That's why we call them 'guardian angels.' See? Yours is right over there, waiting to take you to Earth."

"Hold it," the Little Soul said. "You're telling me I have a guardian angel named Melvin?"

"Well," God said with a wink, "Clarence wasn't available."

"Oh," the Little Soul nodded, pretending to understand, although the Little Soul did not understand at all.

"Melvin will be with you all the time, and he'll explain everything," God assured. "But right now, you have to hurry. Look, your turn is next! You're about to be born!"

And it was true! The Little Soul was only one step away from the Doorway to Earth, and there was no one ahead in line. The Little Soul sang happily, "I get to have a body! I get to have a body!"

"Yes, you do!" God said with a big grin. "Okay then, off you go! Have a wonderful time! And don't forget to call me if you need me!"

And so it was that the Little Soul was born.

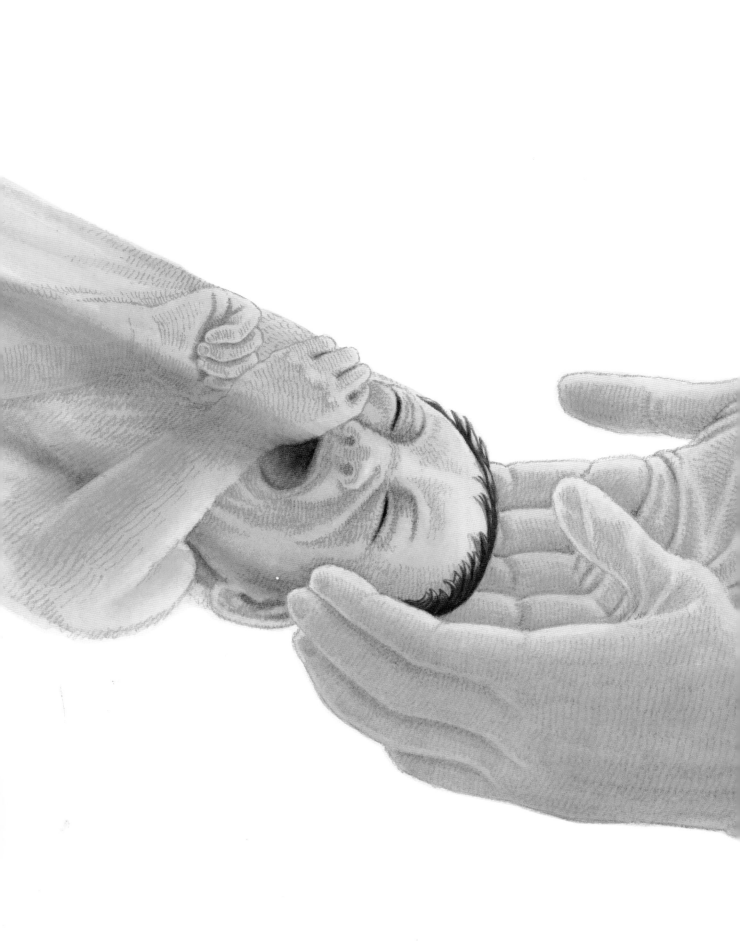

2

"WOW, I'M SOMEBODY!" the Little Soul sang out the moment after becoming a baby. It sounded like crying to everyone else in the room, but the Little Soul was actually singing. "I'm not only a soul anymore! Now I've got a body!"

"Yes! Now you're somebody!" Melvin joined in the singing from across the room. A lot of people were crowding around the baby, and Melvin wanted to make sure they had plenty of space.

Just then the Little Soul heard one of the people say, "It's a girl!" and everyone "oooed" and "aahhed" and some even clapped their hands. "Welcome, Meghan!" said one of them.

"Is that my name?" the Little Soul asked.

"Sure is," Melvin beamed. "Aren't you excited?"

"I am!" the Little Soul replied. "At least, I think I am." She wondered about this because just then she was picked up by someone she didn't even know!

"It's okay," Melvin assured her. "She's a doctor. She's just going to see how much you weigh, and how big you are, and check out your body to make sure that everything is perfect!"

And while the doctor and nurses were doing this, the Little Soul couldn't stop thinking. Finally, she asked, "Is it good to be a girl?"

"Of course it is! It's wonderful," Melvin replied.

"Is it better than being a boy?"

"Nope."

"You mean being a boy is better than being a girl?"

"Nope."

"You mean that neither one is better?"

"That's exactly what I mean," Melvin said approvingly. "And don't ever let anyone tell you anything different."

"Why would anyone want to do that?" Meghan wondered.

"Well," Melvin replied, "some people don't understand what you know now, as a baby. They grow up and they forget things."

"Yeah," Meghan agreed. "Someone was just telling me about how we forget things, but I can't remember who it was . . ."

"I'll remind you later," Melvin promised. "But right now you have to get used to having a body."

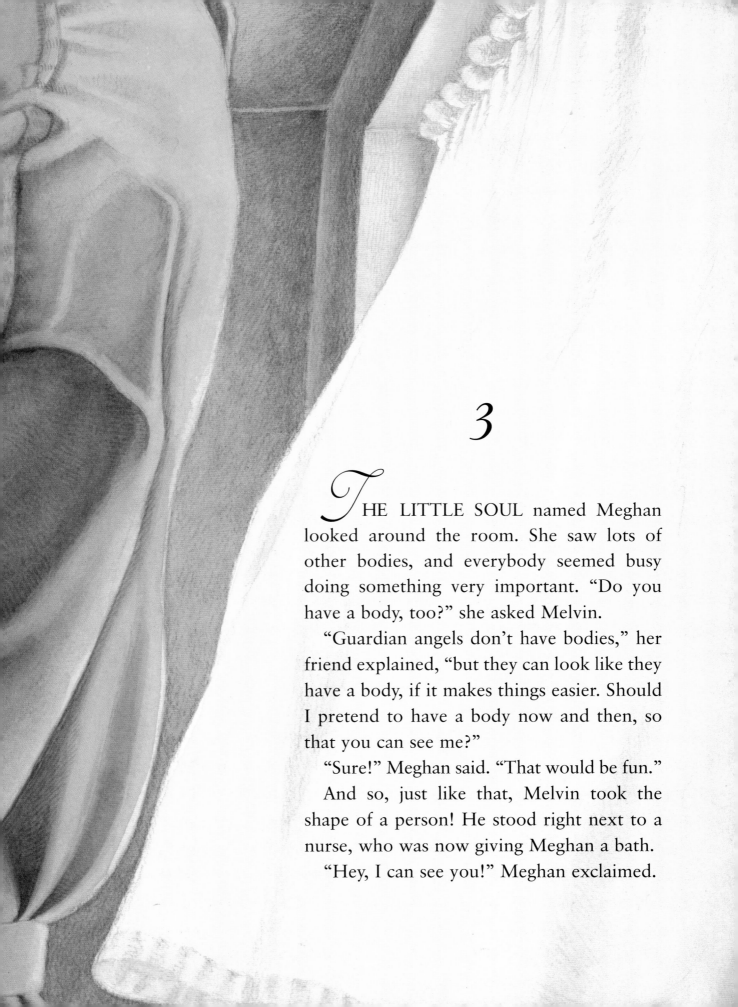

3

THE LITTLE SOUL named Meghan looked around the room. She saw lots of other bodies, and everybody seemed busy doing something very important. "Do you have a body, too?" she asked Melvin.

"Guardian angels don't have bodies," her friend explained, "but they can look like they have a body, if it makes things easier. Should I pretend to have a body now and then, so that you can see me?"

"Sure!" Meghan said. "That would be fun."

And so, just like that, Melvin took the shape of a person! He stood right next to a nurse, who was now giving Meghan a bath.

"Hey, I can see you!" Meghan exclaimed.

"Good. Now try to hold a picture of me in your memory because before too long, you may not be able to see me anymore."

"Why not? Are you going away? God said you would be my special friend forever, and be with me every minute!"

"I WILL be with you every minute," Melvin said firmly. "I'm not going anywhere. But sometimes when you tell other people that you see your 'special friend,' they may try to convince you that I'm not here."

Meghan was amazed. "How come?" she asked.

"Because THEY can't see me, and so they don't believe you're actually seeing me, either. And so they'll say that I'm in your imagination."

"Are you?" the Little Soul blinked her eyes.

"Yes, of course," Melvin answered. "But that doesn't mean I'm not real. Everything in your imagination can be as real as you make it. Always remember that."

Meghan thought about this for a long time. Well, a long time for a baby, anyway—which is about a minute. Then a funny look crossed her face. "Hey!" she said. "This water is getting cold!"

Melvin moved quickly to the nurse. "Oh, my gosh, she made a mistake," he told the Little Soul. "She let the water cool down without adding some warm. I'll see if I can make her think about it." Then Melvin whispered into the nurse's ear.

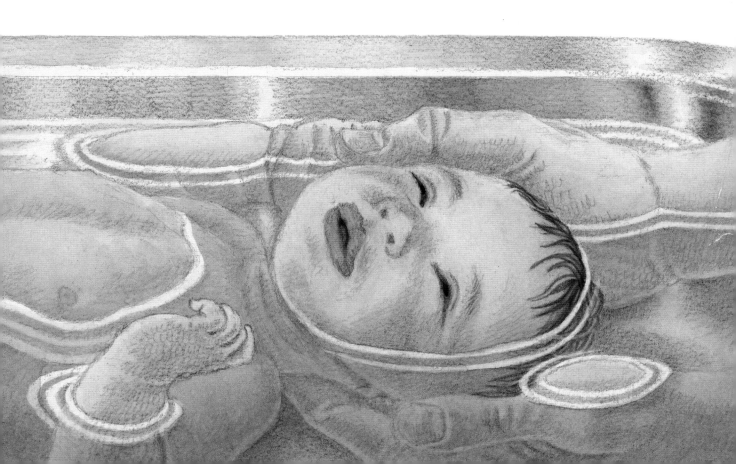

Sure enough, the nurse just at that moment poured some nice warm water over Meghan.

"It was a mistake," Melvin said again. "Will you forgive her?"

The Little Soul thought and thought. Finally she said, "What does 'forgive her' mean?"

It was then that Melvin understood that he was really going to have a lot of work to do! Why, the Little Soul had forgotten why she even came to Earth! She went through the Doorway to Earth and forgot everything! She didn't even remember that she asked to be born so that she could experience what it was like to forgive someone.

(Oh, that's a part of the story that you haven't heard yet, isn't it . . . well, you see, the reason the Little Soul asked to be born was that it wanted to experience what it was like to be forgiving. When it was not living on the Earth, the Little Soul understood that the whole reason anyone even HAD a life was to give them a chance to experience everything! Sooooo . . . the Little Soul wanted to experience forgiveness, and asked God if it could come to Earth in order to do that. But now, the Little Soul had forgotten all about that!)

"I'll tell you about what it means to forgive in just a bit," the guardian angel told Meghan. "It's a pretty big explanation, and you're busy right now."

And she certainly was. The nurse was drying Meghan off with a big, soft towel, and then everyone was checking her hands and her feet and her ears and everything! They seemed pretty happy because everyone was saying, "What a beautiful baby! She's perfect!"

"So," said the Little Soul, "what's next, now that I have a body and know who I am?"

"Who do you think you are?" asked Melvin.

"I'm this, I'm this," Meghan said, pointing to her body. "This is who I am!"

"No, it's not," Melvin laughed. "I know it's who you think you are, but your body is not you, it's yours."

All that Meghan could say was, "Huh?"

Melvin laughed again. "I said, your body is not you, it's yours. That means your body is not who you ARE, it's something you HAVE."

"Like a toy?" Meghan asked.

"Hmmmm," Melvin thought for a moment. "More like a tool, to build something with."

"But what will I be building?"

"A life."

"And just how," asked Meghan, "do I build a life using my body?"

"By experiencing," Melvin responded, sounding very much like a professor in a big college somewhere.

"Experiencing what?"

"Experiencing whatever you want to experience that you can't experience unless you have a body."

Melvin wondered whether the Little Soul would be able to understand.

"Well, I'll tell you what I want to experience right now!" Meghan blurted out, and it's a good thing that guardian angels can understand Babycry because no one else in the room had any idea what she was saying. "I want to experience being warm! I'm getting cold again! I wish someone would bring me a blankie."

And can you believe it? Just then a woman brought over a soft, warm blanket, wrapping it snuggly around the baby.

"Wow! Did you see that?" Meghan cried out. "All I did was wish that someone would bring me a blankie, and a blankie showed up!"

"Isn't that great?" Melvin chuckled softly. "That's how it works."

"That's how what works?"

"That's how life works. You can wish for something and just like 'that' you can get it."

Meghan could hardly believe her ears. "Really?" she asked. "All I have to do is wish?"

"Well, it helps if you wish upon a star," Melvin smiled, "but it's not absolutely necessary. There's only one thing that's absolutely necessary."

"What's that?" Meghan asked eagerly.

"Faith."

"Faith?"

"Yup," Melvin went on. "You've got to believe that you'll always have everything you need. You've got to believe that God is on your side."

Now the Little Soul's eyes opened very wide, and she asked the most surprising question.

"Who's 'God'?"

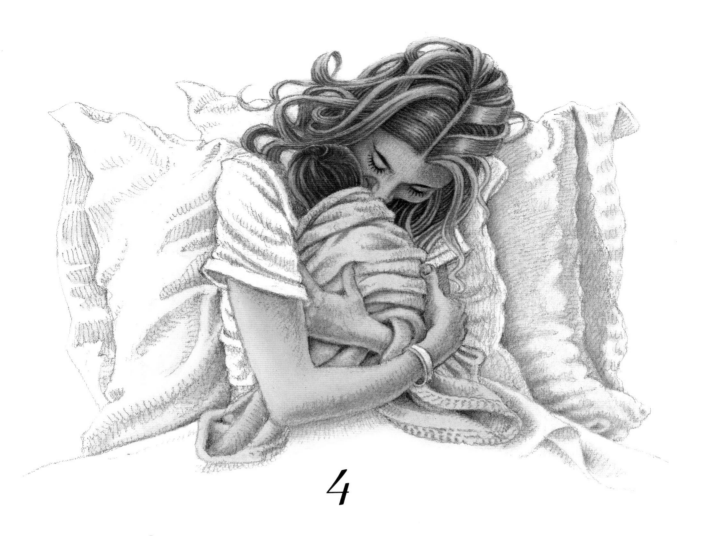

4

MELVIN THE GUARDIAN ANGEL looked down at the Little Soul and smiled the most angelic smile.

"Well, my little Meghan," he whispered gently, "you really have forgotten everything, haven't you? God is the One who put you here, and put me here, and put everything here."

"Really?" the Little Soul asked. "Well, where is she? Tell me more about her!"

Melvin smiled again. But just as he was about to explain all about God, Meghan was being picked up and placed in someone's arms.

"Oh, this is wonderful!" she squealed with delight. "It feels so good to be held here! It feels just like I felt before, when I wasn't born yet! I would know that feeling anywhere! What's it called?"

And Melvin replied, "It's called 'Mommy.'"

And at that very moment Meghan felt a hand touching her face, and a kiss planted right there on top of her head!

"Wow! What was that?" she exclaimed.

And Melvin replied, "That was 'Daddy.'"

"But what was that feeling?" the Little Soul wanted to know. "It's that feeling that I would know anywhere. What's that feeling that I felt when Mommy held me and Daddy kissed me?"

"Love," her angel explained. "That feeling is called 'Love.'"

"Wow, that feels good. How can I get more of that?"

"Oh, that's easy," said Melvin. "Just give it away."

The Little Soul looked at her guardian angel with a big question on her face. "How do I do that?" she asked. "I don't know how to do that. Can you show me how? Can you? Can you?" Meghan pleaded, and she flashed the angel her biggest smile.

"Do you know what's amazing?" Melvin began. "You're doing it right now, just by the way you're looking up at me. Something as simple as how you look at people is a way you can give love away. Just a smile from you, Meghan, is a wonderful gift that makes everyone very happy."

And so, the Little Soul smiled at her mommy and daddy.

"There! You see?" Melvin cried. "Now that made them feel wonderful!" And that was no exaggeration. Meghan's mommy and daddy were both filled with joy, and they smiled right back at Meghan!

"Wow, when I do it to them, they do it to me!" the Little Soul chimed in.

"Yes!" Melvin nodded his head. "That's another secret about life! What you do to others is done right back to you! You're really learning fast."

"This is fun!" Meghan decided. "Are there any other ways to give love away?"

Melvin chuckled. "There are so many ways, you can't even count them!"

"Hey, maybe that's what I can do while I have this body!" shouted the Little Soul. "I could spend this whole lifetime just learning how to love!"

"You certainly could," Melvin agreed. And it was then that the Guardian Angel decided to teach the Little Soul about what it means to forgive. Because, you see, forgiving someone is one of the biggest ways to give love away.

After Melvin helped her understand what forgiveness was, Meghan cuddled in the arms of her mommy, with her daddy giving her hugs and kisses. She decided right then and there to forgive the nurse for all that cold water!

Of course, she wasn't able to talk yet (that would happen many months later and that is another whole story!), so there was only one thing the Little Soul could think of to do to let the nurse know that Meghan forgave her. And do you know what she did?

That's right. She looked right at the nurse and . . .

. . . smiled her biggest smile.

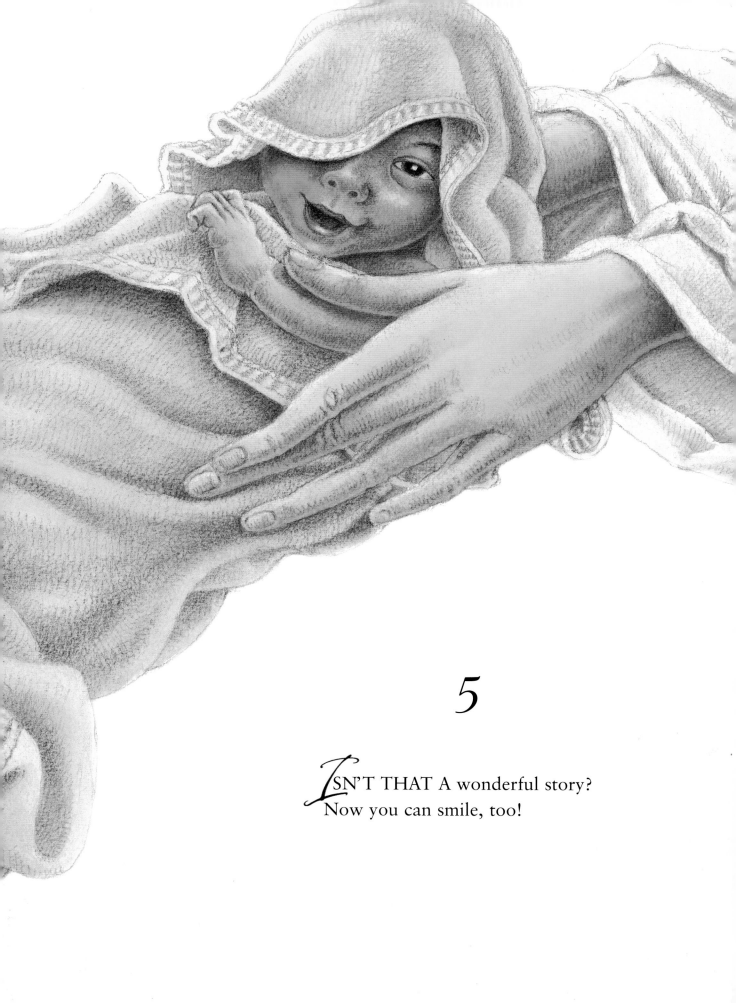

5

*I*SN'T THAT A wonderful story?
Now you can smile, too!

Young Spirit Books

Hampton Roads Publishing Company is dedicated to providing quality children's books that stimulate the intellect, teach valuable lessons, and allow our children's spirits to grow. We have created our line of Young Spirit Books for the evolving human spirit of our children. Give your children Young Spirit Books—their key to a whole new world!

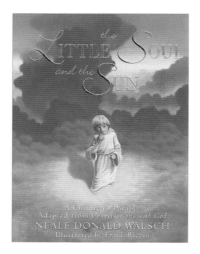

If you enjoyed *The Little Soul and the Earth*, then we recommend the first book in the series, *The Little Soul and the Sun*. It is an enchanting story about simple truths on good and evil, the physical world of duality, and the meaning of love. Look for it wherever books are sold, or check it out on our Web site, address below.

HAMPTON ROADS PUBLISHING COMPANY publishes books on a variety of subjects, including metaphysics, spirituality, health, visionary fiction, and other related topics.

For a copy of our latest trade catalog, call toll-free, 800-766-8009, or send your name and address to:

HAMPTON ROADS PUBLISHING COMPANY, INC.
1125 STONEY RIDGE ROAD • CHARLOTTESVILLE, VA 22902
e-mail: hrpc@hrpub.com • www.hrpub.com